A Note to Parents and Caregivers:

Read-it! Readers are for children who are just starting on the amazing road to reading. These beautiful books support both the acquisition of reading skills and the love of books.

The RED LEVEL presents familiar topics using common words and repeating sentence patterns.

The BLUE LEVEL presents new ideas using a larger vocabulary and varied sentence structure.

The YELLOW LEVEL presents more challenging ideas, a broad vocabulary, and wide variety in sentence structure.

The GREEN LEVEL presents more complex ideas, an extended vocabulary range, and expanded language structures.

When sharing a book with your child, read in short stretches, pausing often to talk about the pictures. Have your child turn the pages and point to the pictures and familiar words. And be sure to reread favorite stories or parts of stories.

There is no right or wrong way to share books with children. Find time to read with your child, and pass on the legacy of literacy.

Adria F. Klein, Ph.D.
Professor Emeritus
California State University
San Bernardino, California

Managing Editor: Bob Temple
Creative Director: Terri Foley
Editor: Brenda Haugen
Editorial Adviser: Andrea Cascardi
Copy Editor: Laurie Kahn
Designer: Melissa Voda
Page production: The Design Lab
The illustrations in this book were prepared digitally.

Picture Window Books
5115 Excelsior Boulevard
Suite 232
Minneapolis, MN 55416
1-877-845-8392
www.picturewindowbooks.com

Printed in the United States of America.

Library of Congress Cataloging-in-Publication Data
Blair, Eric.
The frog prince / by Jacob and Wilhelm Grimm ; adapted by Eric Blair ;
illustrated by Todd Ouren.
p. cm. — (Read-it! readers fairy tales)
Summary: An easy-to-read retelling of the classic tale of a beautiful princess who makes a
promise to a frog which she does not intend to keep.
ISBN 1-4048-0313-0 (lib. Bdg)
[1. Fairy tales. 2. Folklore—Germany.] I. Grimm, Jacob, 1785-1863. II. Grimm, Wilhelm,
1786-1859. III. Ouren, Todd, ill. IV. Frog prince. English. V. Title. VI. Series.
PZ8.B5688 Fr 2004
398.2—dc22   2003014026

PiCTURE WiNDOW BOOKS

The Frog Prince

A Retelling of the Grimms' Fairy Tale
By Eric Blair

Illustrated by Todd Ouren

Content Adviser:
Kathy Baxter, M.A.
Former Coordinator of Children's Services
Anoka County (Minnesota) Library

Reading Advisers:
Adria F. Klein, Ph.D.
Professor Emeritus, California State University
San Bernardino, California

Susan Kesselring, M.A.
Literacy Educator
Rosemount-Apple Valley-Eagan (Minnesota) School

Picture Window Books
Minneapolis, Minnesota

About the Brothers Grimm

To help a friend, brothers Jacob and Wilhelm
Grimm began collecting old stories told
in their home country of Germany. Events
in their lives would take the brothers away
from their project, but they never forgot
about it. Several years later, the Grimms
published their first books of fairy tales.
The stories they collected still are enjoyed
by children and adults today.

Once upon a time, there was a king with many daughters. The youngest daughter was the most beautiful of all.

The princess had a golden ball.
It was her favorite toy. She would
throw the ball in the air and catch it.
She loved this game.

A dark forest stood near the palace.
At the edge of the forest was a well.
The well was so deep, no one could see
the bottom. The princess would go near
the well and play with her golden ball.

One day, the princess was playing near the well. She threw the ball high in the air. She tried to catch it, but she missed. The ball bounced and rolled into the well. The princess started to cry.

Suddenly, a voice asked, "Why are you crying?" The princess looked around. The voice had come from a frog. His fat, ugly head was sticking out of the water.

"I'm crying because my golden ball rolled into the well. I'll never see it again," the princess said.

"Don't cry," said the frog. "I can help you. What will you give me if I get your ball?"

"Anything at all," said the princess.
"Whatever you want. My dresses,
my jewels, even my crown of gold."

"I'll tell you what I want," said the frog.
"Let me be your friend. Play with me.
Let me eat from your plate and drink
from your cup. Let me sleep in your bed.
Promise me these things, and I will get
your golden ball for you."

The princess agreed. "I'll give you anything," she said. But the princess wasn't telling the truth. She was thinking, *This frog is silly. How could a frog ever have a human for a friend?*

The frog dived into the water. He quickly
returned with the golden ball in his mouth.
He spit the ball on the grass.

The princess picked up the ball and ran
into the palace. "Come back!"
the frog cried. "Take me with you."
But the princess was gone. She forgot
about the frog and her promise.

The next day, the princess was
at the dinner table with her father,
the king. She ate from her fancy
gold plate and drank from her fancy
gold cup.

Splish, splash, plop, plop. The frog crawled
out of the well and up the palace stairs.
He knocked on the door.
"Princess, let me in!" cried the frog.

The princess ran to see who was
at the door. When she saw the frog,
she slammed the door in his face.
She came back to the table.
The king saw she was afraid.
"Is there some terrible monster
at the door?" he asked.

"No, Father," said the princess.
"It's just an ugly frog." The princess told
her father about the ball, the frog,
and the promise she had made.

The king said, "When you make a promise,
you must keep it. Let him in."

"But Father, he's so slimy," the princess said.
"How could he be my friend?"

But the princess did as her father ordered
and let the frog into the palace. The frog
followed the princess to the table.
"Pick me up, and put me on your chair,"
the frog said. Again, the king made
the princess do it.

Then the frog wanted to be on the table. "Push your plate closer so we can eat together," he said. The princess did what the frog asked, but she didn't like it. The frog ate lots of food. The princess hardly ate anything.

When the frog was done eating, he said, "Take me to your bedroom. We can lie down and sleep." The princess was afraid to touch the cold, slimy frog. Now he was going to sleep with her in her pretty bed!

23

The princess began to cry. Her father
became angry. "When someone helps
you and you have made a promise,
you must keep it," the king said.

The princess carefully picked up the frog.
She carried him upstairs to her bedroom.

The princess put the frog on the floor
in her bedroom. She crawled
into her bed and turned off the light.

When the princess was in bed, the frog
hopped over and tugged on the sheets.
"I'm tired, and I want to go to sleep.
Lift me up, or I'll tell your father,"
said the frog.

The princess became angry. She picked up the frog and threw him against the wall as hard as she could. "There, you ugly frog. Now you'll sleep," she said.

When he dropped to the floor, the frog turned into a handsome prince. He told the princess a wicked witch had cast a magic spell that had turned him into a frog. He had lost all hope until the princess came to play by the well.

The princess looked into the prince's beautiful eyes. She believed him. The princess let the prince become her dearest friend and husband. They went to his father's kingdom, and they lived happily ever after.

Levels for *Read-it!* Readers

Read-it! Readers help children practice early reading skills
with brightly illustrated stories.

Red Level: Familiar topics with frequently used words and
repeating patterns.

Blue Level: New ideas with a larger vocabulary and a variety
of language structures.

Little Red Riding Hood, by Maggie Moore 1-4048-0064-6

The Three Little Pigs, by Maggie Moore 1-4048-0071-9

Yellow Level: Challenging ideas with an expanded vocabulary
and a wide variety of sentences.

Cinderella, by Barrie Wade 1-4048-0052-2

Goldilocks and the Three Bears, by Barrie Wade 1-4048-0057-3

Jack and the Beanstalk, by Maggie Moore 1-4048-0059-X

The Three Billy Goats Gruff, by Barrie Wade 1-4048-0070-0

Green Level: More complex ideas with an extended vocabulary
range and expanded language structures.

The Brave Little Tailor, by Eric Blair 1-4048-0315-7

The Bremen Town Musicians, by Eric Blair 1-4048-0310-6

The Emperor's New Clothes, by Susan Blackaby 1-4048-0224-X

The Fisherman and His Wife, by Eric Blair 1-4048-0317-3

The Frog Prince, by Eric Blair 1-4048-0313-0

Hansel and Gretel, by Eric Blair 1-4048-0316-5

The Little Mermaid, by Susan Blackaby 1-4048-0221-5

The Princess and the Pea, by Susan Blackaby 1-4048-0223-1

Rumpelstiltskin, by Eric Blair 1-4048-0311-4

The Shoemaker and His Elves, by Eric Blair 1-4048-0314-9

Snow White, by Eric Blair 1-4048-0312-2

The Steadfast Tin Soldier, by Susan Blackaby 1-4048-0226-6

Thumbelina, by Susan Blackaby 1-4048-0225-8

The Ugly Duckling, by Susan Blackaby 1-4048-0222-3

EMPIRE GARDENS SCHOOL
1060 E. EMPIRE ST.
SAN JOSE, CA 95112